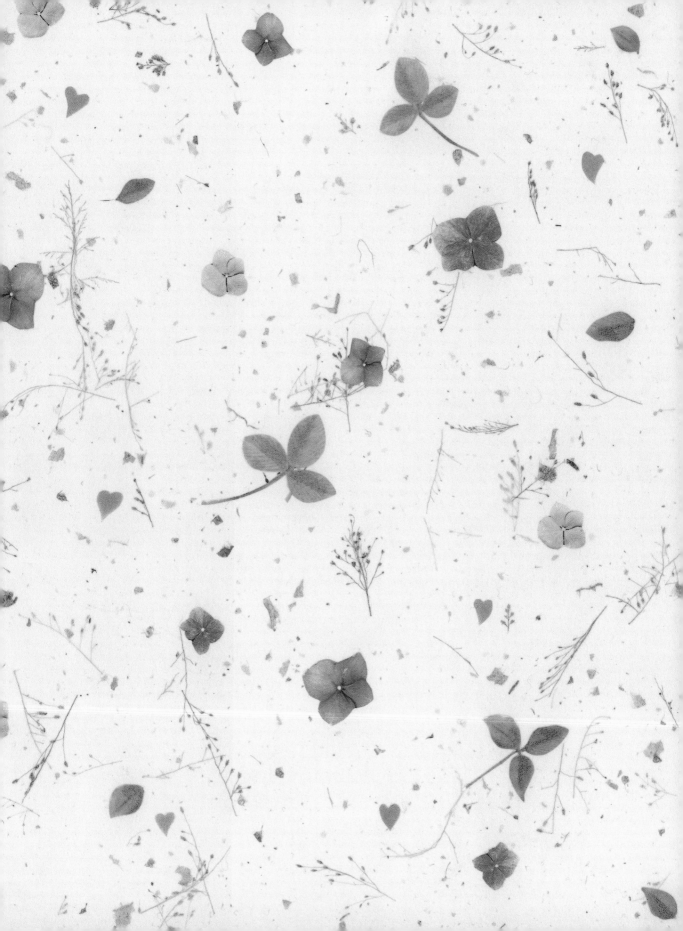

With hoppiness and love to all
the bunny valentines out there—MM

To Ollie and Phoebe—CJC

First published in the United Kingdom in 2006 by Chicken House,
2 Palmer Street, Frome, Somerset BA11 1DS.
www.doublecluck.com

ISBN-13: 978-0-439-74834-6
ISBN-10: 0-439-74834-8

12 11 10 9 8 7 6 5 4 3 2   7 8 9 10 11 12/0

Printed in the U.S.A.   40
First Bookshelf edition, January 2007

Body text was set in Providence. Display text was set in Caterpillar and Litterbox.

Book design by Leyah Jensen

Dear Bunny

BY
Michaela Morgan

ILLUSTRATED BY
Caroline Jayne Church

SCHOLASTIC INC.

New York Toronto London Auckland Sydney
Mexico City New Delhi Hong Kong Buenos Aires

Once upon a time
there were two bunny rabbits.

Their names were Valentino
and Valenteeny—
or Tino and Teeny for short.

ONE LIVED HERE

AND ONE
LIVED THERE

Every now and then
they would peek at each
other and think,
Oh, how lovely that
bunny is!

But neither of them
said a thing because they were both
very, very, very, very, very,
very (very) shy.

One day Tino had an idea.

I'll write a little letter—
just a friendly hello sort of letter—
and I'll put it in the hollow log
for Teeny to find.

This is the letter
Tino wrote:

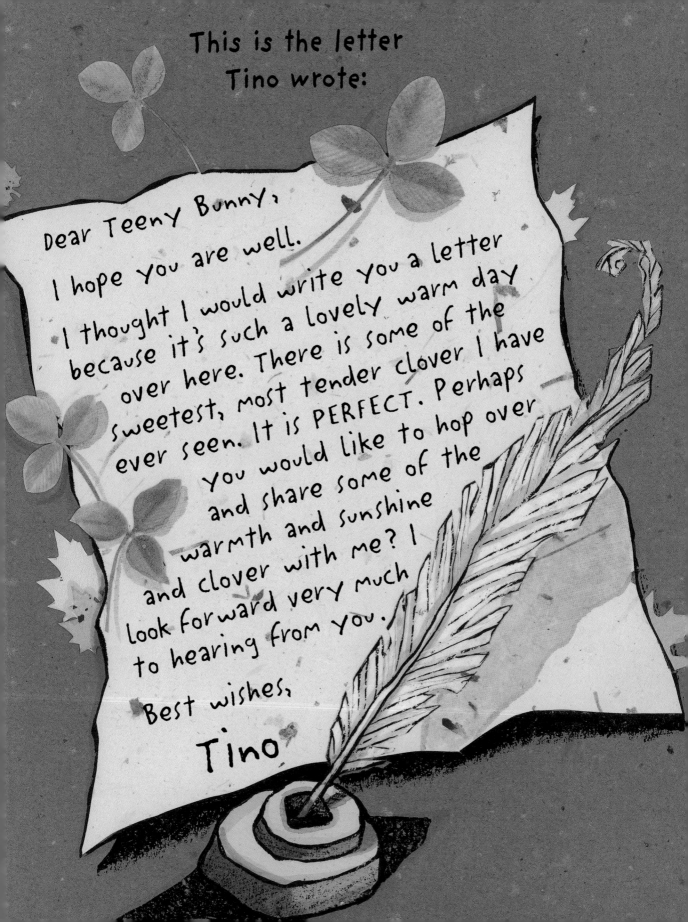

Dear Teeny Bunny,

I hope you are well.

I thought I would write you a letter
because it's such a lovely warm day
over here. There is some of the
sweetest, most tender clover I have
ever seen. It is PERFECT. Perhaps
you would like to hop over
and share some of the
warmth and sunshine
and clover with me? I
look forward very much
to hearing from you.

Best wishes,

Tino

Then Tino went hop-hop-hopping
over to the hollow log and popped in the letter,
just as it started to rain.

A little later, Teeny had the very same idea and so set off with a fine present of leaves and petals and a little note for Tino.

Teeny popped everything into the hollow log and hopped off quickly as the rain plip-plopped down.

This is the note
Teeny wrote:

Dear Tino,

I hope you will like these lovely leaves and petals. They are very beautiful and so very sweet and tender. They have exceptional tenderness. I picked them especially for you. Please accept them as a small gift from me.

Teeny

P.S. I so look forward to hearing from you.

Meanwhile, by the riverbank, the mouse family and their nest were getting wetter and wetter and wetter.

PLIP
PLOP
PITTER
PATTER

SPERLOSH!

To the hollow log!
It was dry and warm and snugly
lined with paper, petals,
and leaves. PERFECT!

All through the cold and stormy days,
the mice snoozed. They were snug and safe
and surrounded by Love and Warmth and
Exceptional Tenderness.

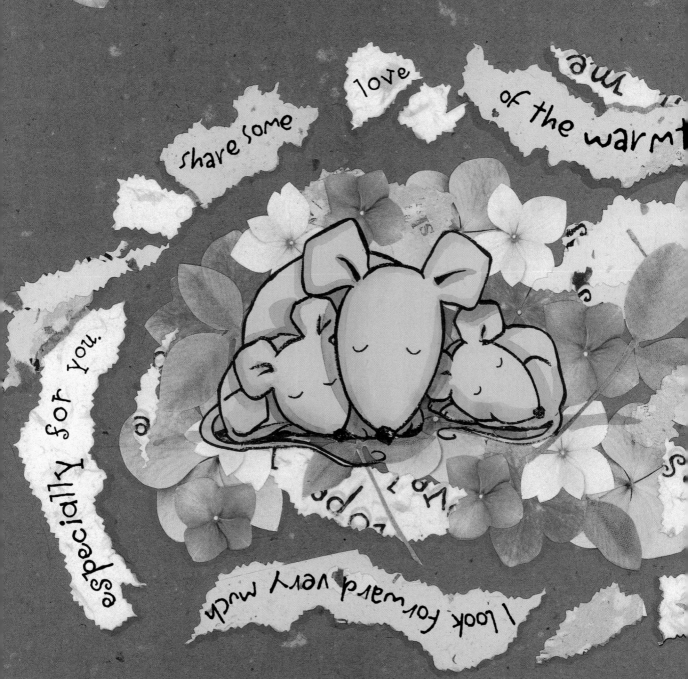

exceptional

some of the sweetest,

tenderness.

PERFECT.

and

sunshy

are very beautiful and

At last, the sun peeked through the clouds and the mice peeked out of their nest.

And what do you think they saw?

And then a little later . . .

"Oh," squeaked Mrs. Mouse. "Oh oh oh!"

"What have we done?" squeaked Mr. Mouse.

"What can we do?" squeaked the babies.

Then, for very small creatures, they had a very

big idea.

tenderness

sweetest,

They decided to give
up their nest, put the words
back together, and make a message
for the lovelorn bunnies. They
would choose only the best words,
the ones that had kept them
warmest through the cold and
stormy days.

especially for you.

most tender

Best wishes,

sunshiney thoughts

most tender love

so lovely

beautiful

exceptionally sweet

and PERFECT

accept

me

Tino hopped over and gazed at it.

especially for you

hope warm wishes ar

for the sweetest Bes

you ar

so

oh so ver

pleas

Teeny hopped over and gazed at it.

sunshiney   thoughts

most tender   love

so   lovely

beautiful

exceptionally sw

and PERFECT

accept

me

Then they gazed
at each other
and that was that . . .

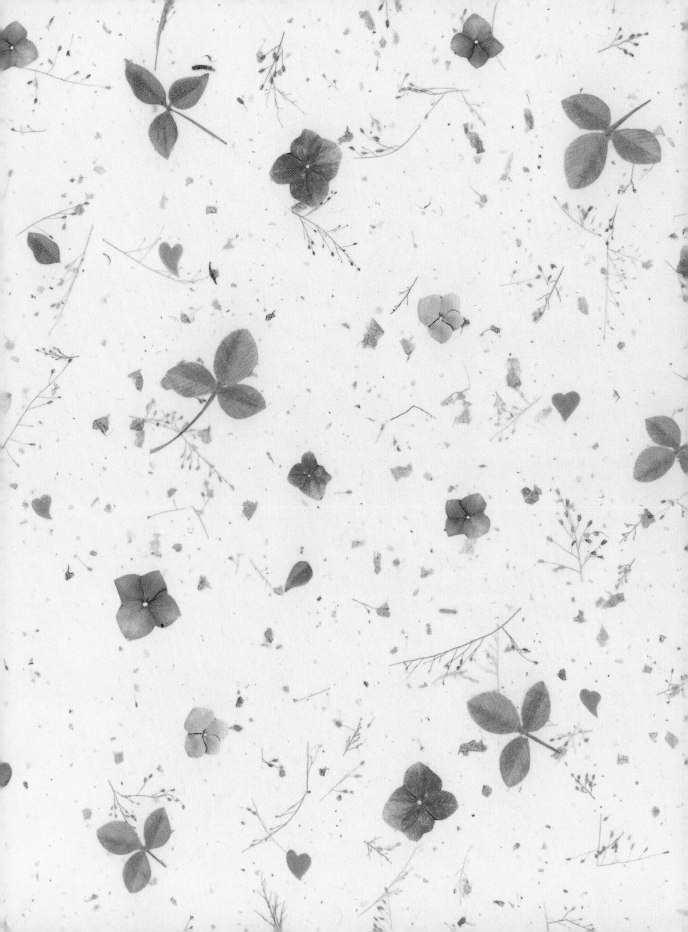